New Clothes for New Year's Day

By Hyun-Joo Bae

Kane/Miller
BOOK PUBLISHERS

Today is New Year's Day.

It's a new year,
it's a new day, and
it's a new morning.
It's the first day for the beginning of everything.

The new sun hasn't shown up, and there are new clouds in the sky.
(I hope we have new snow, too.)

But the very best new things of all the new things are…

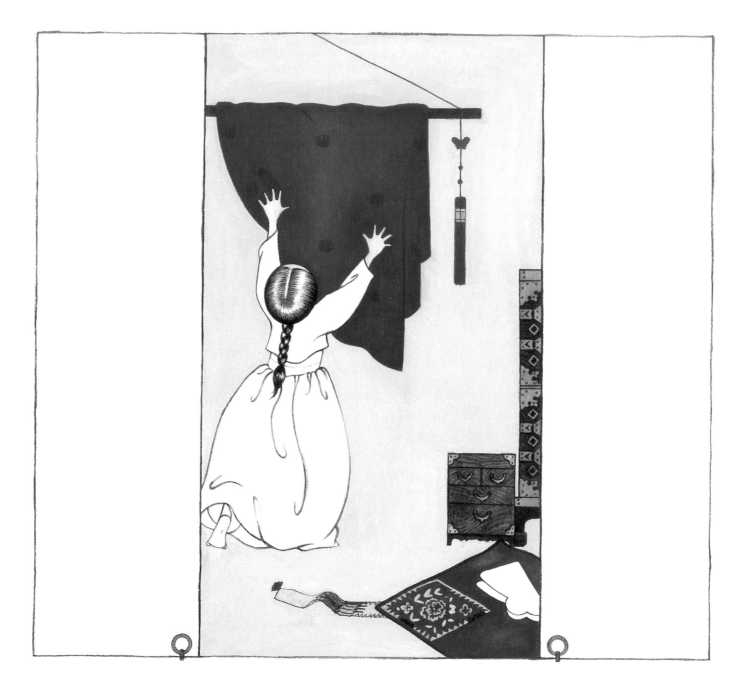

My new skirt and jacket!

Mother made new clothes for New Year's Day.
Aren't they beautiful?

A crimson silk skirt.
A rainbow-striped jacket.
Delicate socks embroidered with flowers.
A hair ribbon of red and gold.

I could hardly sleep last night.

But today I finally get to wear my wonderful new clothes. Finally!

Stretch on tiptoes to reach the hanger...
"Umph!"

Hold one side in each hand, then

arms spread wide, wrap the crimson skirt around,

take the sash and tie a knot.

One after the other

put on the cotton socks with their red-flower embroidery.

Make sure the designs are in the right place.

Oomph!

Whoops!

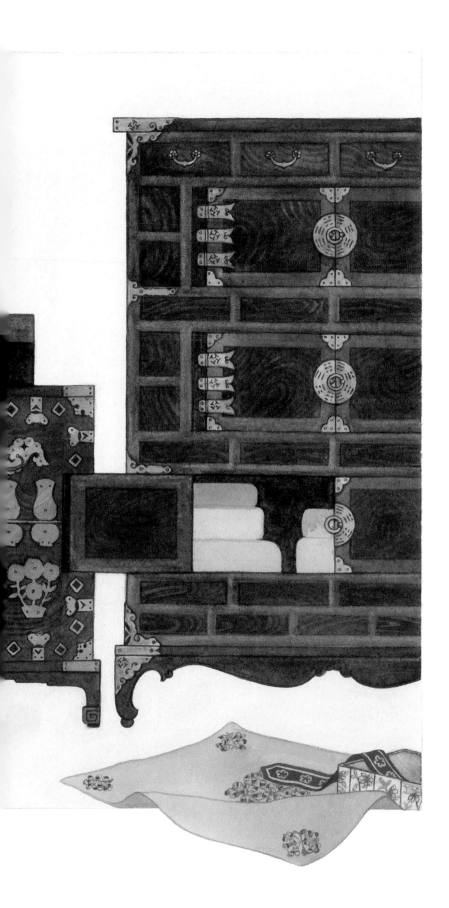

Arms go in carefully,

one at a time,
into the rainbow-striped jacket.

Pull the right side first and
cover it with the left.

It may be tied tightly (how pretty!)
or left untied.

Put a head band on over neatly braided hair.

In front of the mirror, fasten the hair ribbon of red and gold…

Ahhhh! It's not easy!

That's pretty.

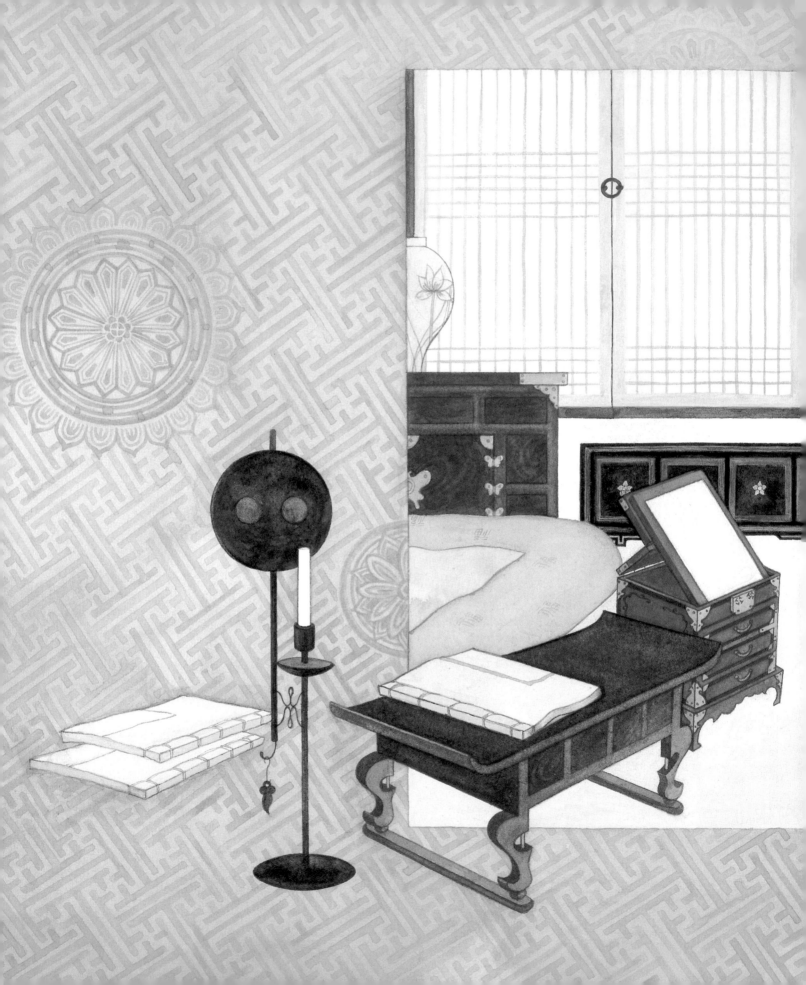

Time for the flowered shoes, a gift from Father,

and the warm, furry vest with the gold decorations.

Plus a special winter hat, to help keep warm.

Put on the new shoes,
the new flower-embroidered shoes,

the dazzling new shoes (they fit perfectly).

Slip on the furry vest.

Hang a charm and a lucky bag on the jacket string.

It's good luck!

Put on the black satin winter hat.

Everything is new, from head to toe.

A New Year, a new day, a new morning.

New clothes.

We start the year with new things.

New things, for the year-older me.

Time to go…oh!

New snow for New Year's Day!

The perfect day to make New Year's calls
and to wish everyone good luck in the New Year.

New Year's Day

New Year's Day, celebrating the start of the Lunar New Year, is one of the most important holidays in Korea. New Year's Day starts earlier than most days. Families rise early, hold a ceremony to honor their ancestors, give the first bow of the New Year and eat rice cake soup for breakfast. The soup is very important because Koreans do not count age on their birthdays, but on New Year's Day. They become one year older only after they've eaten this special soup. After breakfast it's time to get together with relatives and wish each other a "Happy New Year," as children give a bow (Se-bae) to their elders. There are also special new clothes for New Year's Day (Sol-bim), and it's a lot of fun to wear them while making New Year's visits and New Year's bows.

Dressing Up

Of all the new clothes worn on New Year's Day, those worn by children are especially beautiful. Shall we take a look at the new clothes the little girl in this book wears? She wears a crimson silk skirt, a rainbow-striped jacket and a furry vest. She puts on cotton socks and shoes, both embroidered with flowers. She also wears a headband and ties a hair ribbon of red and gold to the end of her braid. Her hat protects her from the cold as she makes her New Year's visits. She also has a lucky charm and bag to hang from her jacket string. If she had a brother, he would be dressed in clothes just as beautiful as hers – special pants and jacket (Baji Jeogori), a hat (Bokgeon), a coat (Kkachi Durumagi) and an overcoat (Jeonbok).

Significance

In the past, women used to make their family's special New Year's clothes with great care and devotion. That is why the clothes for New Year's Day are not only beautiful but also hold special meaning. For example, the colors in the rainbow-striped jacket represent things such as water, fire, metal, wood and earth. The striped pattern represents the wish that the wearer be in harmony just like the harmonious colors. The embroidery on the socks is for good luck. The bat embroidered on the charm (蝠) is in Chinese character, which has the same pronunciation as 福 ("luck" in Korean). The new clothes the little girl in this book is wearing have all these elements. We can tell that her mother is very good at sewing, and that her family is wealthy enough to provide a charm and a pair of flower-embroidered shoes. This doesn't mean though, that everyone's new clothes need to be this fancy. What matters most is the meaning of the new clothes, even if they are plain – the maker's wish for the wearer to forget unhappy events of the previous year and to have a Happy New Year, and the wearer's resolution to be a better person in the New Year as he or she turns one year older. That is what "New Clothes for New Year's Day" means.

❶ SAEKDONG JEOGORI
A jacket made of colorful fabrics.

❷ NORIGAE
A charm that hangs from the jacket.

❸ CHIMA
A crimson silk skirt with a 福 ("luck" or "bliss") pattern.

❹ BAESSI DANGGI
A decorated headband.

❺ TTITDON
A special ornament to link the charm to the jacket.

❻ JUMEONI
A round-shaped lucky bag (like in this illustration) is called Durujumeoni, while square-shaped lucky bags are called Gwijumeoni.

❼ JOBAWI
A hat worn to keep warm.

❽ BEOSEON
Cotton socks.

❾ KKOTSIN
Leather shoes covered with embroidered silk.

Kane/Miller Book Publishers, Inc.
First American Edition 2007
by Kane/Miller Book Publishers, Inc.
La Jolla, California

Originally published as "The New Year's Best Clothes"
© 2006 by Bae, Hyun-Joo
This translated edition is published by arrangement with Sakyejul Publishing Ltd.,
through Shinwon Agency Co.
English edition © 2007 by Kane/Miller Book Publishers, Inc.

Special thanks to Mihee Kim

Library of Congress Control Number: 2006931560
Printed and bound in China
2 3 4 5 6 7 8 9 10

ISBN: 978-1-933605-29-6